For the love I see, everywhere.
In everyone.

Contents

Love

27.09.23

Show me your sharpest thorns, and I'll show you skin
ready to bleed. Just let me hold you, my flower.

16.09.22

He makes trees want to hug him,
and makes the wind want to never stop dancing.
He makes the rain swim with the sea,
and leaves the sun, happily prancing.
He makes the soil want to kiss his feet.
Makes the flowers wish they were held.
He makes the moon sad that it is so far,
and he makes me the luckiest girl in the world.

22.11.22

I fell in love with her pink nose,
puffed lips,
and her saddened eyes.

I loved the way she relied on only me for strength:
to stay alive;
for food,
for bathing,
for shelter.

I loved the way her head was always in a dream,
she was never fully awake.

Never really there.

I loved her holding me,
well trying to.
I loved her fragile kisses and hugs.

I loved her bad breath,
as she hadn't found the will to taste toothpaste in a
week's time.

3

I loved her knotty hair,
clumped in the shape of her pillow.

I loved her tears,
and her voice,
and her harmed wrists.

I loved the fact that her heart was pouring with
pain,
and I was the only one she truly missed.

I loved that nothing could make her worse than she
already was.
I grew to love her pain more than anything else.

For now, I am no longer depressed and it's scary as
hell.
                    -Falling in love with your depression.

24.10.23

I wonder when we will finally meet, my love.
I am watering my flowers, everyday
to greet you with gardens.

12.10.23

I hold my own heart.
I tell her:
I love you,
I chose you,
I hear you.
It's bleeding.
All of this time I thought it was needing another.
Maybe she just needs herself.
I love you.
I love you.
She is confused,
used to fill the void with men's conditional love,
which is so stupid.
Because what can a man do for me that I can't?
You beat for me.
You are mine,
before you are anyone else's.
Beat for me.
Cry for me.
Bleed for me.
Smile for me!
Smile for me, pretty.
Become mine fully.

Stop looking for the kiss of another.
I'll kiss you forever.
I promise I will.

5.12.22

<u>The ocean's lover</u>
The waves consume her, briefly
and she does not resist.
She sits with comfort
as the water soaks her face.
She exhales slightly deeper
if she is fully submerged.
But regardless of what happens,
her softness is present.
She doesn't flinch if a wave hits her too hard.
She doesn't show grace as the strong tide is washed away.
She becomes one with the water,
as the water falls in love with her.
She stares for hours
at the life in the waters
and the sea wonders
why a woman with so much to live for
watches the motions of the waves,
as if *that* is her whole life.

12.02.21

I didn't mean to fall in love.
But I don't think I ever really fell,
for that would hurt me
and you'd never allow that.

No,
I walked,
step by step,
blindly following your lead
knowing that as long as I am with you,
I will always be safe.
And my heart,
she will always be protected.

26.02.21

Let me crawl under your skin, and live there.
Only then will I be satisfied with your touch.
(Maybe).

15.11.23

Tell me,
how have you managed to steal my heart
through your words alone?
Every word like honey dripping from your lips,
every word like a beautiful song.
You are a beautiful song,
I never want to stop listening to.
I'll listen over and over again.
Write the lyrics obsessively over my walls.
Engrave its name onto my skin.
Take the guitar with me wherever I go.
I need you wherever I go.

14.08.23

She was one of my blindfolded masterpieces.
I do this
to make an unbiasedly beautiful woman.

I don't allow my preferences to interfere with my art
work,
instead I allow my hands to just work its magic.
It is just like clay, really.

It was within the first hour that I noticed simply how
much she would amaze me.
You might think that I'm exaggerating, but if you
simply saw her, you would understand.
And I don't mean to say:
see her- face or body.

Yes,
her every curve, every bone, her every feature is
beautiful.
Each piece of flesh sculpted by an angel's hand.
But that is irrelevant to her actual beauty.

The most beautiful thing a human being can have,
her soul.
Ethereal.
Unique.
My favourite creation yet.

-   What I imagine God's thought process was, as He
    was making her.

I want to love and protect every human being in
this world.
I want to kiss strangers on their foreheads
and make every child smile.
I want to heal every broken man and woman.
I want to touch their wounds and get their blood
on my hands,
as long as I am able to heal them.

I want to kiss every person's heart until it stops
bleeding. I want to stroke every person's face, until
the tears stop streaming.

I am okay, I know how to be. I know how to heal.
A lot of people are so broken and do not even know
where to start.
I just want to make them feel the love that they
deserve,
Because every single soul
is so so beautiful.

I know that ugliness exists in the world,
for I've had a taste of hell.

But even then,
I know that the people hurting,
are bleeding their wounds,
on to strangers who were never responsible for their
pain,

and

I feel love within me,
so deeply,
so often
and I think that my purpose in life is to love the world.

Because if a single act of kindness
can save a soul,
I want to save billions.

31.07.21

All of my problems
are drowned out from the sound of your
voice. And when you leave,
they come crashing back,
fiercely,
like waves.

18.10.23

Dark red nails and black eyes,

But my soul is cotton

And heart is ice.

His hands are so warm

And my heart, she melts:

every

single

time.

17

The absence of love

26.02.22

You told me to dance
so I am barefoot, doing ballet on the dance floor.
The ground is made of shredded glass,
and my feet are getting so sore.
They say beauty is pain
yet you only admire me when I am blue,
or cut, or bruised.
You seem to like mental scars too.
I thought that I gave you life,
seems like you feed off of mine.
Everytime you hold me,
and pretend that we are fine,
I want to cry,
I want to scream
but 'it is not how it may seem'.
It is all in my head.
You don't even exist.
I am sure you'll one day disappear,
if I keep telling myself this.
Yet everytime I wake,
you're the first thing I see
until you decide to beat me so hard,
everything is just bloody.

27.01.23

The darkness never scared me.
As a child, it was the dark night that rocked me to
sleep,
rather than my mother's arms.
It was the darkness that wiped my tears as sadness
consumed me.
It was darkness that gripped my father's hand and
pulled him under.
It was the darkness of the earth I wanted to
decompose within.
So I grew to be comforted by the dark.

Until I met a boy made of light.

Who burned away everything that I've ever known
so bright he was fire.
He illuminated my whole life
but just like fire,
if you get too close,
if you dare to love it,
you burn
and I often burned
but I would allow it.

I let him within my four dark walls
I needed him, to see.
He poured love into me and
I couldn't understand why,
but that didn't matter,
for now
I see
that
the world isn't consumed by darkness.
It was just my mind that was.

20.05.22

I eat
so much
to try to feed
the hole in my heart
maybe if I stuff food in to it
it will be full one day
but right now
all it's doing,
is making my stomach sick.

My lips are blue
My tongue numb
Eyes are full of blood
Before its tears start to come
My heart so sore
My chest so tight
My scabby hair
Not parted right
My lungs are full
And my breath stops
Out of confusion
My mind starts to knot
My blood external
Sick on my skin
This is the aftermath
Of everything within
My body scarred
My throat near slit
I hold myself
I start to sit
I ask the world
Before I go insane
Do I need to be this way
For you to see my pain?

10.09.23

Feeling like I'm floating
with no one to ground me.
Feeling inadequate as the
walls have gotten further.
Feeling so small
but simultaneously like I'm taking up
the world's space.
Planning on my every move
instead of flowing with grace.
Racing heart
but I try to calm her down.
It can be a whole lot worse
I just want it to be better now.
The awkward stage of thinking you're about to
drown
still holding my breath because
I have hope.
I know God will send me waves
tears down my cheeks mixed
with the saltwater.
I've been learning to surf, God
you'd be proud.
I've been learning to surf, dad

you'd be proud.
Missing his arms missing his frown,
sometimes that comfort feeling
is what's keeping you down,
sometimes the familiar is holding me down
but he's so familiar,
and I love his smell.
Would I rather stay with the familiar
or go through hell?
But the question should be
would I rather stay with the familiar
and go through hell?
Would I rather stuff him in my heart
trying to make him fit in
this dad shaped hole?
Would I rather just die?
Is there any purpose to it all?
But
it's not death I want
but the ending of suffering,
the death of pain,
the birth of happiness,
and can I be happy
when stepping into the unknown?

I only know so much
am I really ready to let go?
If it's a feeling I'm chasing
I'll never be high
what more can this man give to me
for me to not say goodbye?
Is this self sabotage or self love?
Is this the man I'm dreaming of?
Is this the life I've been afraid of?
Is this all there is to love?
Am I ready to spend my whole life trying to be
understood?
Is it worth the struggle?
So many questions,
but spent my whole life
never trusting
my own voice so now she is silenced
but was it anxiety or intuition?
How would I ever know?
What would I ever do?

29.10.23

I wanted you to be mine so badly.
Even with a ring on my finger
My name tattooed on your flesh
Even with your skin on mine
Holding you so close your breath became
my breath,
Even when our skeletons merged with one
another,
And our skin was tangled to one,

Our hearts were worlds apart.

No matter how hard I tried
You could never be mine.

29.10.23

What is the purpose of my days
If there is an absence of love?
I decide to embody it
For if it hasn't found me yet
I should become it.
And maybe he will seek
And love will be hereafter.
As long as we become it.

29.11.23

I used to rip my hair out,
When you would call my name.
Shivers down the spine,
And butterflies no longer looked the same.
And so I put shredded glass in tonight's
dinner.
You always grab another plate.
Would laugh and call yourself greedy,
You always grab my face,
Would lick it and call yourself needy.
You took the knife after you was done
with your meal,
Held it to my throat,
And fucked me to your appeal.
I'll never forget.
And when your organs were slowly
Bleeding out from the digested shredded
glass,
I felt no shame
I used to rip my hair out
Everytime you called my name.

Everything in between

04.09.23

She bathes her body in sunlight,
coconut oil dripping from her bare skin.
She inhales the scent of roses,
and exhales the weight in her heart.
She listens to the sound of the birds that are
singing in her ear.
She chooses to focus on the good.
She chooses to focus on the love.

She sits naked on the earth's grass
she allows it to tickle her bare skin
aware of its dirt,
but focusing on its softness
she chooses to focus on the love.

The wind is growing cold
as it wraps itself around her chest.
She chooses to focus on the sun's warmth,
she chooses to focus on the love.

Heart feeling heavy
as her mind takes her to the past.
Reminiscing of all the wrongs in her life
but she's trying to focus on the now.

She is trying to focus on the love.
She chooses to focus on the love.

Her stomach has been empty for days
but she focuses on her heart being full.
She focuses on the good.
She chooses to focus on the love.

And maybe she'll spend her whole life trying
and maybe it'll forever feel like a choice.
Maybe someday
she'll finally turn the screams in her mind into a
loving voice
as she focuses on the love.
Thank God for my own love.

05.12.22

The smallest trigger
Makes my head spin for days
Thoughts swallowing me whole
Mind constantly aches
Heart constantly races
Constantly lie awake
It's constant for days
Constant
Make it go away.

Everytime baby Sarah fell,
her mama would pick her right up
and kiss her
and Sarah had noticed that the pain would always go
away.
Now, at the age of 5
Sarah sits,
legs crossed
with a mouth covered with blood
she's desperately kissing her mother's stab wound
and cries,
'Why isn't it getting better, mama?'.

03.11.23

There are fragments of liquid gold in the rain
As it drenches my naked body.
This is the way I bathe,
Through water, so holy.

Glistening waves,
The sea wraps itself around me,
Flowing through and through
Slowly purifying me.

Pluviophile doesn't begin to describe
The love I have as it pours.
Heaven speaks in purls
And when she speaks, she roars.

And when the rain stops singing
And the petrichor is all that remains,
I thank the universe
As I am made of mostly water,
Just like the beautiful rains.

23.09.20

If you are tired enough,
Sleeping on rocks can feel like clouds.
If you are desperate enough,
Being with evil,
Can feel like love.

09.12.19

'I'll hurt anyone who hurts you', I promised.
Her eyes finally lit up after hours of pouring pain.
Her shoulders relaxed and she let out a breath I didn't
even realise she was holding in.
She needed to hear those words, you could tell.

Now, with curiosity, her eyes travel down to my palm.
'I did say that I'll hurt anyone who hurts you.'
I explain, after seeing the fresh cuts.
Her cheeks now full of life,
As it pours out of her wrists.
It was too late.
My grip was tight,
My hand trembling,
But I knew I had to keep my word.
She needed this, I told myself
As I held the gun against her head.

If you think I will sit here
and turn a boy into a man.
Think twice.
I've done that before: spent my years teaching him
how to be.
Moulding him with my very own hands.
Now he's a piece of art for another,
but if you look within him
you see glimpses of me.
To make a boy into a man, I have the ability.
But, when I see little boys trying to be my man,
I sit them down, and hold their fragile hands:
tell them to think twice.
Call me when you are grown,
and maybe then we can converse,
for I refuse to teach little boys to be men.
I am not their mother.
I am Mother Nature, the universe.
I am God's tear of happiness,
I am everything because of me,
and I look at your desperation to befriend me
with deep empathy.
but honestly,
I would rather be alone then be in your half-arse
company,
so if you think I will sit here
and turn a boy into a man
ever again: Think twice.
I only like to be with men, you see.

10.11.23

<u>a single thought</u>
I realise that everything is but a thought
and the tears that stream down my face
no longer feel genuine.
A single thought
can make my heart ache
but in reality
nothing has changed.
So when I get a thought,
that tells me how much I miss you
I almost feel ashamed,
because in a moment's time
I shift my focus
and suddenly you're insane
and I'm the one
that got away.
So if a single thought
can make my heart break,
a single thought
is all that it takes to
make the pain go away,
so with a single thought
you no longer exist
and my life is perfect in every single way.

26.09.23

Everything was happening fast:
The thoughts, the feelings, the hurt
I was in deep pain,
continuously.
Luckily after every shot, things slowed
the once chaos turned to calmness
the once devastation turned to drunkeness
and suddenly
no one was against me anymore.
It was me and the world
not the world against me.
I felt good.
Things were good.
Too good.
Then the ringing started
that stupid fucking ringing
in both ears
louder than police sirens
louder than the music
fuck, it was louder than the thoughts to begin
with.
And I knew I had to go home
I needed to rest.

And so I
tumbled through the door
and that's when I saw her body.
What was she doing on the floor?
Only then did I notice the blood seeping out of
her head
vigorously, desperately,
continuously.
The puddle was huge
how did I not immediately notice?
It was me being slow.
And suddenly I wished things were fast again
as I wait for the ambulance to come
and bring back the life of my mum.

19.01.24

It frightens me to believe that feelings
are temporary
others compare sadness to the rains
but as a child who was delivered in rainstorms,
I thought that soaking from the clouds tears,
was the skys version of sane.

It poured for the most of my childhood
I wish it was a lie
it was rare to see
a crystal clear, blue sky

and when it stopped raining
I was surrounded by the angry seas
fleeing our home country,
with a boat full of refugees.

Our boat would rock left to right
as the sky would loudly yell
I held my mama's hand tight,
I hadn't known this sky very well

our boat would shiver with fear,
every time we heard a roar
and the sea would help itself
on to our wooden floor.

The skies were still grey,
and angry with lines,
so I prayed and prayed
to see that familiar rain just one more time

and once we reached shore
(I couldn't believe that we did)
the sun didn't come out,
in fact for days it hid.

It rained and rained
but this time I didn't mind:
for once, we had warmth
and shelter when we dined

and when people tell me
like the rain,
the sadness will go away
I don't believe them
but make space for the feeling everyday.

For the problem isn't
the rainwater
it's the fear of drowning,
anyway.

Acknowledgements

Psa: The dates at the top are when each poem is written.

Thank you to every person I have ever loved, for allowing me to write this book. Thank you to every person who hurt me, as without you I wouldn't have experienced the deep wounds that ignited my passion to write to begin with.

A lot of my work comes from the traumatic events in which I experience or encounter. A lot of the time, I find that I am putting myself within other's shoes, when they are going through something so disastrous, and this is when I find myself creating the most bittersweet, and impacting work. This book is very much like a forbidden journal of my own and other's experiences.

On one hand, I hope you, as a reader, can find some truth within my work, and relate to some of these experiences because I know the satisfaction one feels when they see their life being written by a stranger. However, on the other, some of these poems are extremely burdening things to be able to relate to, so if you do, I am sorry. And, I love you.

Thank you to my dad, thank you for always pushing me to achieve what my heart desired, and for reminding me that, 'My hard work will always pay off'. I know you would be proud, and probably concerned, reading this baba.

Thank you to my mother, who does the best she can every single day to ensure me and my siblings' are happy. Thank you for telling me: 'Let your soul be as beautiful as your looks.'. I am who I am, thanks to you.

Thank you to my absolute best friend, Nazar. I hope you recognise yourself in these poems, because you are absolutely everything I know about love. You make my heart so full, and I thank Allah you exist, daily.

And thank you, dear reader, for allowing me to share my limited experiences of the world and love with you.

With love, always

Naz

Printed in Great Britain
by Amazon

39393654R00056